Haley and Bix

Best Friends, No Matter What

by
SCOTT HIGGS

Scholastic Canada Ltd.
Toronto New York London Auckland Sydney
Mexico City New Delhi Hong Kong Buenos Aires

For Haley and Bix
— S.H.

The illustrations in this book were inked by hand,
then scanned, coloured and shaded in Photoshop.

The text type was set in 20 pt Maiandra GD.

Scholastic Canada Ltd.
604 King Street West, Toronto, Ontario M5V 1E1, Canada

Scholastic Inc.
557 Broadway, New York, NY 10012, USA

Scholastic Australia Pty Limited
PO Box 579, Gosford, NSW 2250, Australia

Scholastic New Zealand Limited
Private Bag 94407, Greenmount, Auckland, New Zealand

Scholastic Children's Books
Euston House, 24 Eversholt Street,
London NW1 1DB, UK

Library and Archives Canada Cataloguing in Publication
Higgs, Scott
Best friends, no matter what / Scott Higgs.
(Haley and Bix)
ISBN 0-439-94725-1 (bound). — ISBN 0-439-94750-2 (pbk.)
I. Title. II. Series: Higgs, Scott Haley and Bix.
PS8615.I37B48 2006   jC813'.6   C2006-900814-0

6 5 4 3 2 1   Printed in Canada   06 07 08 09 10

Haley and Bix were very different.

Haley loved to play rough games.
She liked to tackle things.
She liked to roll in the muck.

Bix enjoyed the quieter side of life.
She liked things to be tidy.
She liked things to be pretty.

Haley had a stuffed puppy
named Scraps.

Scraps had pine needles stuck in his fur.
He smelled a bit like peanut butter
and old socks.

Bix had a stuffed puppy named
Jessie Flower.

Jessie Flower always looked perfect.
Once a month Bix gently wiped her
clean with a soft cloth.

Even though Haley and Bix were very
different, there was no doubt about it.

They were best friends.

One day Bix had some bad news.

"Mom and Dad said we have to move to Italy for a year."

Italy was far away across the ocean.

Haley and Bix had never been apart
for a whole year before.
This was very bad news indeed.

The girls tried to stop Bix from leaving.

Their plan didn't work.

At the airport, Haley
tried to sneak along
in Bix's suitcase.

That didn't work either.

"Don't worry, Bix! I'll find a way to keep us together!

I promise!"

Bix went to Italy, but Haley did not give up.

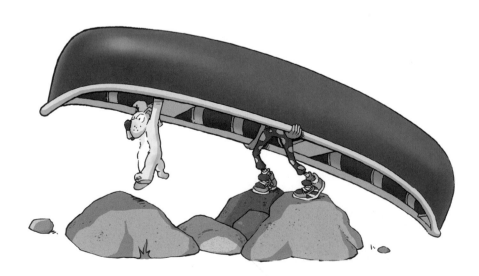

Instead, she tried and tried to get to
Italy by herself.

Haley had some very good plans . . .

but nothing seemed to work.

Haley missed her best friend.
She had never felt so lonesome.

Across the ocean in Italy, Bix was feeling lonesome, too.

Then one day, a package arrived at Haley's house.

Haley tore open the box. Inside was a big surprise.

It was Jessie Flower!

That same day, a package arrived at Bix's house in Italy.

Bix opened her package very carefully.

There was Scraps smiling up at her!

Haley dressed up Jessie Flower in her
finest ribbons and had a fancy tea party.

Everything was just the way Bix
would have liked it.

Bix and Scraps ran in wild circles all around the living room.

It was just what Haley would have done if she'd been there.

Before they knew it, Haley and Bix were not so lonesome anymore.

Haley had a little bit of Bix to hold on to.

Bix had a little bit of Haley.

And both girls knew it would not be such a long year after all.